SUBMARINES
AT SEA

RICHARD AND LOUISE SPILSBURY

PowerKiDS
press

New York

3 9082 13653 5716

Published in 2018 by **The Rosen Publishing Group, Inc.**
29 East 21st Street, New York, NY 10010

Cataloging-in-Publication Data
Names: Spilsbury, Richard. | Spilsbury, Louise
Title: Submarines at sea / Richard and Louise Spilsbury.
Description: New York : PowerKids Press, 2018. | Series: Machines at sea | Includes index.
Identifiers: ISBN 9781499434545 (pbk.) | ISBN 9781499434491 (library bound) |
  ISBN 9781499434392 (6 pack)
Subjects: LCSH: Submarines (Ships)--United States--Juvenile literature.
Classification: LCC V858.S65 2018 | DDC 623.825'7--dc23

Produced for Rosen by Calcium
Editors for Calcium: Sarah Eason and Jennifer Sanderson
Designers for Calcium: Paul Myerscough and Jennie Child
Picture researcher: Harriet McGregor

Photo Credits: Cover: Adam K. Thomas, U.S. Navy. Inside: National Oceanic and Atmospheric
Administration/Department of Commerce: OAR/National Undersea Research Program (NURP),
Woods Hole Oceanographic Inst. 20; Shutterstock: Alexyz3d 17, Biggunsband 10, Danilo Ducak
7, Everett Historical 9, Thomas Koch 12, Dai Mar Tamarack 25, Prawat Thananithaporn 14; Royal
Navy/Ministry of Defense: LA(Phot) Will Haigh/MOD 31, CPOA(Phot) Thomas McDonald/MOD
28, POA(Phot) Tam McDonald/Crown Copyright 5; U.S. Navy: Mass Communication Specialist
2nd Class Gretchen M. Albrecht 18, Journalist 3rd Class Wes Eplen 19, Mass Communication
Specialist 2nd Class Ronald Gutridge 11, Chief Photographer's Mate Andrew McKaskle 15,
Mass Communication Specialist 2nd Class Ricardo J. Reyes 21, Josn Brandon Shelander,
USN 13, John F. Williams 29; Wikipedia: Bluefin/Mierlo 27, Leonard G. 8, Brennan Phillips 26,
Wahrig2003 23.

Manufactured in China
CPSIA Compliance Information: Batch BS17PK: For Further Information contact Rosen Publishing, New York, New York at 1-800-237-9932.

SUBMARINES AT SEA

UNDERWATER BOATS

Submarines are remarkable boats that move through oceans mostly unseen. This is because they are designed to travel underwater. They allow people to survive, explore, and attack from beneath the waves.

Why Underwater?

With high waves and wild winds, oceans can be rough places for ships to travel. The waves and winds can make surface ships buck up and down, and these ships need to use a lot of engine power to cut through the waves. Moving through the calmer waters below the surface is much smoother. Being underwater also keeps submarines hidden. In the past, submarines were used mostly for surprise attacks on enemies.

The problem with being underwater is that it is a difficult environment for humans to cope in. Unlike fish, we cannot breathe oxygen **dissolved** in water, so we need to take air supplies underwater with us. It can also be very dark underwater, as parts of the oceans are far from the sunlit surface. One of the biggest challenges of being underwater is **water pressure**. The push of water is greater the deeper underwater we go.

FIRST SUB

In 1620, Cornelis Drebbel built the first submarine. His submarine looked like two wooden rowboats clamped together and was covered with waterproof, greasy leather. It had two pairs of oars sticking out of the sides with which people inside could row. The Drebbel carried up to 16 passengers and could remain a few feet underwater for 3 hours.

A big submarine is all too obvious at the surface but can soon disappear into the deep, dark ocean.

Parts of a Submarine

The main parts of a submarine include the hull, conn tower, hydroplanes, and engines.

Hull: This is the main waterproof and pressure-proof part of a submarine. The hull contains the passengers, cargo, and weapons.

Conn tower: This is where crew "conn," or control, the submarine.

Hydroplanes: These are fins on the stern (rear) and conn tower or bow (front), which help keep the submarine stable in the water and control its movements up and down.

Engines: The engines are used to move the submarine through the water.

FORCES
UNDERWATER

Submarines stay and move underwater because of forces. These are pushes and pulls that act on objects to make them move or stay still.

Floating and Sinking

The two main forces on any boat are **gravity** and **upthrust**. The **weight** of a submarine is caused by the downward pull of gravity from Earth on its **mass**. Upthrust is the upward push on the ship from seawater below its hull. A submarine can float at the surface because its upthrust exceeds gravity.

Floating is also to do with density, which is the weight of a certain volume of a substance. A hollow submarine has a lower density than the volume of seawater that it **displaces**, so it floats. A submarine sinks because its density is controlled by pumping seawater on board into **ballast tanks**. This increases the weight without affecting the volume of the submarine, so the overall density increases. Once its density is greater than seawater, the submarine sinks. It can rise again by blowing **compressed air** into the ballast tanks, pushing out some heavy water.

The Shape of the Ship

When a submarine uses the **thrust** of its engines to move forward, its **drag** slows it down. Submarines have a teardrop shape, with a tapering bow and stern, and few parts sticking out. This **streamlined** shape reduces drag because water flows more easily past the hull's surface than a squarer, rougher shape.

The hydroplanes are shaped like short airplane wings. When water flows over them at speed, they lift the submarine in the water. This is because the push of water beneath the wing is higher than that on top. The crew changes the angle of the hydroplanes to make the submarine rise or descend at a steeper angle.

NO ROLLING OVER

Many submarines also have vertical fins or tail planes sticking up at their stern. These help stop the submarine from rolling to the sides because their wide surface area is pushed equally by water on either side.

Big, fast submarines have rounded bows to push through the high-pressure water around them.

BUILT FOR DEPTH

Submarines are designed to operate in the depths of the sea. Their thick metal hulls are tough enough to keep their shape when the extreme water pressure could cause them to cave in.

Water Pressure

The deeper a submarine goes, the greater the mass of water above it. This weight explains the rising water pressure. Water pressure usually doubles with every 30 feet (9 m) a submarine descends. This push is strong enough to squeeze water through any gaps and crack normal glass. Submarines have hulls that are welded together tight, so there are no gaps. Any windows are made of thick plastic that does not crack.

Underwater objects feel the same push of water pressure all over: top, bottom, and sides. The best shape for a submarine to survive high pressure is a sphere, but spheres are not very streamlined. To solve this problem, a submarine is circular in cross section, but it has pointed ends to the hull for streamlining, not resisting pressure.

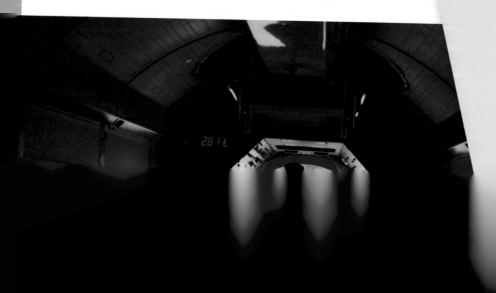

Submarines have a rounded shape to resist water pressure. Air pumped inside keeps the air pressure at a comfortable level for passengers and crew.

In emergencies, submarines rise so fast to the surface to get the crew to safety that they breach, or rise, above the water like giant whales.

Hull Inside a Hull

Submarines have two hulls. The inner hull is the pressure hull. It has **hemispherical** ends to withstand pressure better than the outer hull's pointed ends. The pressure hull protects the crew inside from high pressure and from the very cold temperatures in deep water. This is possible because there is an air gap that helps prevent heat passing out into the water.

Many submarines are warships that may be fired upon. They risk being attacked by enemy **torpedoes**. With a double hull, if the outer hull is pierced, the inner one may remain intact. Then seawater could not flood in and increase weight so much that the submarine can never surface.

KEEPING IN TRIM

Submarines have trim tanks inside, between the hulls. These ballast tanks are at the front and rear of the craft. The crew adjusts the tanks to keep the submarine level in the water and so that the bow falls or rises before the stern during maneuvers.

SUBMARINE POWER

A submarine's thrust is supplied by its large **propeller**. When this set of curved blades spins around, it pushes water backward from the stern. This creates an equal and opposite force from the water behind the ship.

Electric-Powered

Most submarines are electric. Their motors work and spin the propellers using power from giant batteries. Submarines cannot operate using normal gasoline or diesel engines like those used on large ships and trains. These engines use oxygen from air to burn fuel, which releases energy, turning propellers. Submarines are underwater where there is no air, apart from that which is carried on board. If engines used up air, there would be too little for the crew to survive.

The batteries run down during use. So these submarines recharge them using power from an electrical **generator** connected to diesel engines. Crew members turn on these engines only when the submarine is at the surface, when they can use air from outside the boat.

The propeller, or screw, on this older submarine is the width of the boat itself.

Nuclear-Powered

Many large military submarines have **nuclear reactors** on board. These contain special metals that react, releasing large amounts of heat. This heat is used to make high-pressure steam. The steam rotates fan-shaped **turbines** that spin generators, producing power for the electric motors.

Life Support

Electricity from engines is also vital for supporting the crew on board submarines. It powers scrubbers, which are machines that remove poisonous quantities of carbon dioxide gas from the air that the crew exhales (breathes out). Machines are also used to remove salt from seawater, pumped in from outside, to make fresh drinking water.

On big submarines, there are often two steering wheels. One controls the hydroplanes beneath the conn tower, and the other controls the rudder and tail planes.

STEERING

The crew steers the submarine by controlling a large, vertical blade just behind the propeller called the **rudder**. Shifting the steering wheel right twists the rudder right. This increases the surface area the propeller pushes against, so the submarine stern moves left, pushing the bow to the right.

SEEING UNDERWATER

On a submerged submarine, the crew can scan the water's surface for enemy ships with just the tip of a **periscope** breaking the waves. Periscopes work up to 60 feet (18 m) underwater.

Tube Vision

A periscope is a long tube with angled **prisms** at either end. Light from the outside hits the top prism, travels through the dark tube, and reflects off the lower prism into the viewer's eyepieces. **Lenses** inside can magnify and brighten the image so the crew member inside can see clearly. He can rotate the periscope to get an all-around view.

Periscopes are so long that they can be in the way inside the cramped interior of a submarine. Some submarines now have electronic periscopes called **photonic masts**. These use digital cameras to view the scene at the surface to send images to a screen through fiber-optic cables.

Crew members look into an eyepiece to see through the periscope and turn it side to side using the folding handles on the sides.

The screens in the sonar room display what different sonar sensors are locating in the ocean around the submarine.

Sight with Sound

Sunlight does not travel far through water. It is twilight beyond the depth of 600 feet (183 m) and completely dark below 3,000 feet (914 m) or so. The crew "sees" its surroundings using sonar. Sonar is a system that produces sound waves that radiate out from the submarine. When the waves hit an object, they bounce back or reflect as echoes. The system listens out for echoes. It can use the echoes to determine the size of objects in the water, and also how far away they are and how fast they are moving. Sonar can detect anything from whales and enemy submarines to underwater mountains that the submarine should not crash into.

PINPOINT LOCATION

Global Positioning System (GPS) compares the position of an object on Earth with those of 24 different **satellites** in space. A **receiver** on the submarine compares the time a signal was sent by each satellite to the time it was received. The time difference tells the GPS receiver how far away each satellite is, and the system shows the ship's location on an electronic map.

13

HUNTERS OF THE OCEAN

The navies of the world operate two main types of submarine. The first kind are known as hunters. These submarines prowl through the oceans ready to attack the enemy and carry out other military activities.

Underwater Defense

Hunters are nuclear-powered submarines that can stay at sea for 3 months at a time. They have advanced, long-range sonar to seek enemy ships and submarines. Hunters can speed along at around 28 miles per hour (45 km/h), which is nearly four times the speed of the fastest human swimmer.

Their main weapons are torpedoes. Hunters have between four and eight torpedo tubes. These can fire out torpedoes weighing up to 2 tons (1.8 tonnes), which can zoom through the water toward targets up to 30 miles (48 km) away. Each torpedo has built-in sonar to seek its target. It has enough power to blow enemy submarines and ships out of the water.

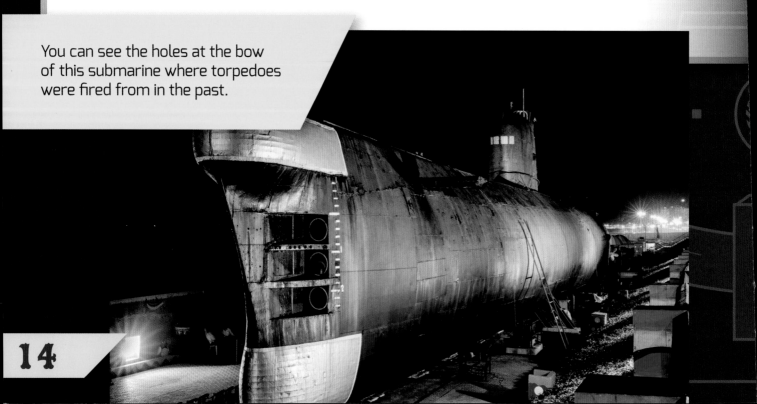

You can see the holes at the bow of this submarine where torpedoes were fired from in the past.

Different Tasks

Hunters are not all about hunting the enemy. They also carry out **surveillance** of enemy forces from the sea. Technology on hunters is also used to check the coastlines of countries where military action might take place, so that the armed forces on ships know where to land. Hunters spot enemy mines (underwater bombs) to help surface ships avoid them, too.

Hunters can also carry naval special operation forces. These are specially trained marine troops who secretly carry out missions on land from the sea. They leave the submarine through hatches or sometimes aboard small torpedo-shaped submarines, which are fired out through torpedo tubes.

Naval special operation forces sometimes leave a submarine at speed in a minisub fired from a torpedo tube.

U-BOATS

In World War I, the destructive power of submarines on ships was first demonstrated. German submarines called U-boats torpedoed and sunk thousands of Allied ships. They sank more than 400 in April 1917 alone. After that, many navies made sure they had submarines in their fleets.

MISSILE LAUNCHERS

The second group of naval submarines have the nickname "boomers." This is because their job is to carry rocket missiles on board, ready to launch from vertical tubes on the top side of the hull at distant enemies.

Guided Missile Submarines

Some boomers move through the oceans with more than 100 Tomahawk missiles ready to fire. These missiles can strike at enemies hundreds of miles inland with great accuracy. Tomahawks are launched from their tubes by a push from compressed air. At the surface, they switch on their rocket engine. This engine burns fuel to push out hot gases for thrust through the air. The Tomahawks open up their wings to fly, too. They are a type of **guided missile** because they have computers on board programmed with the GPS location of a target. The computer controls the missile's flight to make it fly toward that location.

Weapons Not for Use

Some boomers carry missiles with **nuclear warheads**. These are terrifyingly powerful and destructive weapons of war. The weapons are part of the **nuclear deterrence** that many countries have and hope never to use. Boomers with nuclear warheads put off, or deter, countries from launching their own nuclear warheads because if one country fired these missiles, the other would fire back.

Cruise missiles with these warheads can be fired at targets up to 7,000 miles (11,265 km) away from a submarine and fly at over 13,000 miles per hour (20,921 km/h). They are designed to fly up to the edges of space and then fall in arcs toward their targets.

STEALTHY SUBS

Boomers avoid being spotted by enemy sonar because they have special surface coatings on their outer hulls. These include rubber tiles and special plastics. The coatings absorb sound waves from sonar systems, so there are weaker echoes, and they mask the sound of the engines that some sonar systems listen out for underwater.

A guided missile flies skyward from the deck of a submerged boomer submarine.

INSIDE A NAVAL SUBMARINE

A hunter or boomer submarine is operated by up to 140 crew members. The crew lives in cramped conditions together for months at a time, mostly cut off from the surface.

Front of the Boat

The front end of a submarine is where the crew sleep, eat, and where most of the sailors work. They move between levels inside and along the submarine's length through narrow corridors and up metal ladders. Each member sleeps on a narrow bunk or rack. The crew eats in small galleys, where chefs prepare large amounts of energy-rich foods.

Although space is very limited on board a submarine, crew members can always get a little privacy.

The front of the boat also contains the weapons rooms. The crew checks tubes, torpedoes, and missiles, so that they are ready to be launched if needed. The conn tower high above the front end is where the submarine commander or captain works to control the boat. He issues orders to crew to maintain or change direction or speed of the submarine, using GPS information and maps. The conn crew liaises with sonar specialists, who scan the oceans for other boats from a separate, quiet room.

Engine Rooms

The engine rooms are at the back of the submarine. Many crew members keep these machines working properly. The nuclear reactor needs supervision day and night to make sure that the heat it produces is controlled. If these devices get out of control, they can overheat, the fuel can become dangerous to health, and the submarine will be in danger. The crew performs regular drills, practicing to put out fires and dealing with engine and life support emergencies, so that they are ready if problems do occur.

SUBMARINE LIFE PRESERVER

If a submarine loses power, it may sink to great depths, making it dangerous for the crew to swim out. The only possible help is a rescue submarine known as a deep submergence rescue vehicle (DSRV). It can attach to an escape hatch on the stricken submarine to evacuate up to 24 crew members at a time.

The DSRV can be taken near submarines by getting a piggyback ride on another submarine.

UNDERWATER EXPLORATION

People explore underwater for different reasons. Some study shipwrecks, which tell us interesting information about history. Some study the mysterious animals that live in the deep. Others take samples to study water pollution or **global warming**.

Science at Sea

Water pressure, the lack of oxygen and light, and the threat of dangerous animals means it is unsafe for divers to be underwater for very long or to dive very deep. In a submarine, scientists can sit in safety for hours on end and use computers and cameras to record anything they see. Submarines that are used for exploration are often small, sometimes carrying only two people. They have a large, rounded plastic window at the front and other windows for people to see as much as possible outside the vessel.

An exploration submarine like this one has around seven different propellers. These can be used to hover in the water, maneuver over rugged seafloors, or rest on the bottom of the seafloor.

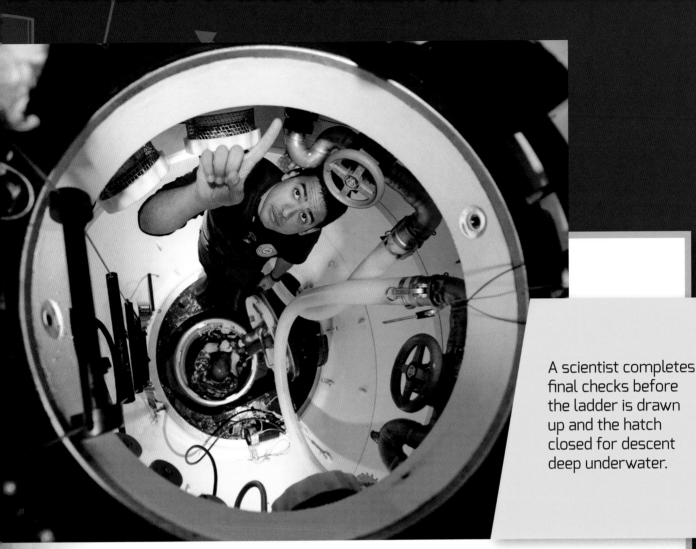

A scientist completes final checks before the ladder is drawn up and the hatch closed for descent deep underwater.

Collecting Data

From inside the submarine, scientists can control video cameras that record what they see, lit up by lights attached to the outside of the submarine. Images and data (information) can be sent straight to computers on a ship at the water's surface. They also have at least two robotic arms attached to a frame on the outside of the submarine. These can use different tools to collect different kinds of samples as the people inside drive the submarine around.

TOOL TIME

Exploration submarine arms use suction pumps to gently collect samples of soft-bodied animals like jellyfish. They can use bottles to collect water samples. They have scoops to gather samples of sand and gravel from the seafloor, plus tools that do many other jobs.

DEEPEST SUBMARINES

Only two submarines carrying people have so far made it to the deepest, darkest depths of the oceans. The Mariana Trench in the Pacific Ocean is the deepest trench in the world. One of its valleys is named Challenger Deep, and it is 6.8 miles (11 km) below the surface.

Reaching Challenger Deep

The first manned vessel to reach Challenger Deep was the *Trieste*. Engineer Auguste Piccard invented this two-man submarine. He and his fellow passenger, Captain Donald Walsh of the US Navy, sat inside a small metal sphere that was part of the hull. This helped them survive the pressure when they traveled down deep. The pressure was the equivalent of having 48 jumbo jets sitting on the craft. This observation chamber was attached to the bottom of a tank filled with gasoline. Gasoline is more buoyant than water and is very hard to compress. This made it ideal for the high pressure of the *Trieste's* deep-sea mission.

Deepsea Challenger

In 2012, filmmaker and explorer James Cameron became the first person to complete a solo submarine dive to Challenger Deep. His submarine was called *Deepsea Challenger*, and the trip took 2 hours and 36 minutes. While he was down there, Cameron used the submarine to gather data, specimens, and images of this foreign world.

The *Trieste* was known as a bathyscaphe, which means "deep ship."

THE CHALLENGE OF THE DEEP

To go down that far, *Deepsea Challenger* had more than 1,000 pounds (450 kg) of steel plates attached to it to help it sink. Once the submarine was deep enough, the plates dropped off, so that *Deepsea Challenger* would float to the surface again.

UNDERWATER TOURISM

Many people want to see the hidden world that lies underwater. They want to witness for themselves the fascinating creatures, colorful coral reefs, and spooky shipwrecks that are found in the deep, dark depths. Some submarines are designed to take tourists underwater.

Built for Pleasure

Tourist submarines are expensive to build because they have to be very safe and have space for a large number of passengers, who must all be able to see outside the submarine as it goes along. They have air conditioning to ensure that the air inside is pleasant to breathe. Tourist submarines also have to operate all year round in most places, so they have be extremely durable. They must also have a large battery capacity to allow for up to ten dives each day and to allow for the extra use of air conditioning.

View of the Deep

There are only about 30 tourist submarines in the world. Some can carry up to 60 people. As well as pilots and crew, they have more than 40 seats along their length. Each seat is next to a viewing window, so passengers can see the underwater world around them as the sub dives. For comfort, the passenger area is usually spacious and more than 6 feet (2 m) high, so that passengers can walk or stand in it. Some submarines have a fully transparent (see-through) glassed cabin, so that people can enjoy panoramic views of the underwater world. At least one member of the crew is usually a scientist who can identify the creatures the passengers see.

Trips underwater usually last about an hour. On this trip, tourists are able to see an underwater shipwreck.

DIVING DEEP

Tourist submarines generally go to a depth of about 120 feet (35 m), but some go as far as 330 feet (100 m).

25

ROBOT
SUBMARINES

Even in a submarine, studying or working deep underwater puts humans at risk. Underwater robots are increasingly being used to explore the ocean depths instead.

Remote Operated Vehicles

Many underwater robots are known as remote operated vehicles, or ROVs, because they are controlled by people sitting in the safety of a ship at the water's surface. They are usually programmed by remote control or by a computer. They are often connected to a ship at the surface by a group of cables, called an umbilical, that supply the robot submarine with power.

ROVs usually have robotic arms that can be fitted with tools such as cutters and grippers. Some tools are tiny and can get into tight spaces, such as inside shipwrecks, but others are the size of a car and are very strong. They can do tasks like holding heavy metal pieces of oil rigs together, so that divers can assemble them.

Robot submarines go deep, so that their human operators do not have to put their lives at risk.

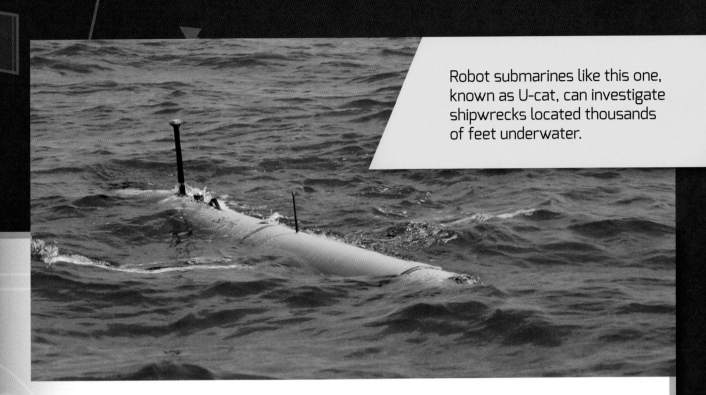

Robot submarines like this one, known as U-cat, can investigate shipwrecks located thousands of feet underwater.

Underwater Operations

Some robots can be preprogrammed to do a task. These include underwater robots that are sent below the ocean to investigate crashed airplanes. Some other robots can be controlled in real time by their operators. These robots have lights and cameras, so operators at the surface can see around the robot. The operators can control the ROV to do many tasks, such as laying communication cables on the ocean floor. They also have a variety of different sensors. Sensors are devices that can, for example, sense chemicals and temperature in water, and objects that the ROV bumps into. Many ROVs are small enough to drive inside things, such as shipwrecks, to study them.

AUVS

Some robot submarines are shaped something like underwater airplanes and are not attached with umbilicals. These are types of autonomous underwater vehicles, or AUVs, that travel the oceans on routes programmed into their computers or by following sound-producing beacons on the seafloor.

SUBMARINES OF THE FUTURE

In the future, submarines will continue to be an important part of international naval fleets defending different countries and groups. That is because they are hidden underwater and can conduct surprise attacks and watch enemies from a distance. They will also remain a vital technology for underwater study, rescue, and leisure. However, there could be many changes made to the underwater boats of the future.

Robot Fleet

The success of ROVs and AUVs (see pages 26–27) in performing underwater tasks is making many experts believe that future navies will include many more of them in their fleet. Underwater robots could be used to detect enemy submarines, while being trickier to spot themselves than large submarines.

And these underwater robots are likely to be networked together. What one robot senses will be communicated to others in the network, so that they can act together in a similar way to how individual bees behave in a swarm. Submarines could even act like underwater aircraft carriers, from where the robots are launched.

Submarines will continue to patrol, defend, and observe the underwater world for years to come.

Submarines in Bubbles

Future submarines could travel as fast as rockets in the air by moving in bubbles. The force of drag slows today's submarines even if they have very streamlined hulls. A device in a submarine's stern could eject gas to make a giant bubble around the boat. Then its hull would not be making contact with the surrounding water, so there would be no drag. However, with no water touching its rudder, the submarine would not be able to steer. This means that it would also be able to release a liquid coating over itself that could supply pressure on the rudder, so that it could work.

LIKE A JELLYFISH

Future submarines might move like jellyfish. These animals squeeze muscles in their body to push out bursts of water. Scientists have discovered that a submarine moves forward with less energy by shooting out bursts of water behind it, rather than a continuous water jet.

This is a competition for designing human-powered submarines. How do you think submarines of the future will move through the water?

GLOSSARY

ballast tanks Spaces that can be filled with water to add weight to a boat.

compressed air Air at high pressure, usually stored in metal bottles.

displaces Pushes aside.

dissolved Mixed completely with a liquid.

drag The force of friction between a moving object and the substance, such as water, through which it moves.

generator A machine that converts spinning movement (mechanical) energy into electrical energy.

Global Positioning System The system to locate position on Earth by comparing it with positions of satellites in space.

global warming Increase in the average Earth temperature resulting from the use of fuels by people.

gravity A downward force pulling any object on Earth's surface or in its atmosphere toward our planet.

guided missile Flying bomb controlled by a computer.

hemispherical Shaped like half a sphere.

lenses Shaped pieces of glass to bend or focus light.

mass The amount of matter in an object.

nuclear deterrence The idea that in a conflict one side will not use nuclear weapons because they will have nuclear weapons used against them.

nuclear reactors Machines that use controlled reactions of nuclear fuel to produce heat used to operate engines.

nuclear warheads Explosives made from nuclear materials fitted to missiles.

periscope A tube-shaped device to see objects above the level of direct sight.

photonic masts Electronic replacements for periscopes that use images from digital video cameras.

prisms Glass devices used to change the angle of light moving through it.

propeller A machine with angled blades that spins to create thrust in water or air.

receiver A device that receives electrical or other signals.

rudder A device that is twisted to make boats change direction.

satellites Objects in space often used for helping communications on Earth by passing on information.

streamlined Describes something that is shaped to reduce drag when moving through water or air.

surveillance Watching people secretly, often to see if they are a threat.

thrust A pushing force in one direction.

torpedoes Missiles that travel to their target underwater.

turbines Fan-shaped machines that spin fast to operate machinery when pushed by moving gases or water.

upthrust A force, also known as buoyancy, that pushes up objects in liquid.

water pressure The push of water on the surface of any object.

weight The effect of gravity on the mass of an object.

FURTHER READING

Books

Farndon, John. *Stickmen's Guide to Watercraft*. Hungry Tomato, 2016.

Resler, T.J. *How Things Work*. National Geographic Children's Books, 2016.

West, David. *Submarines*. Smart Apple Media, 2016.

Websites

Due to the changing nature of Internet links, PowerKids Press has developed an online list of websites related to the subject of this book. This site is updated regularly. Please use this link to access the list: www.powerkidslink.com/mas/submarines

INDEX